INDOMITABLE

INDOMITABLE

TERRY BROOKS

Subterranean Press 2012

First Edition

ISBN
978-1-59606-307-5

Indomitable first appeared in *Legends II*,
edited by Robert Silverberg.

Subterranean Press
PO Box 190106
Burton, MI 48519

www.subterraneanpress.com

T

HE PAST is always with us.

Even though he was only just of an age to be considered a man, Jair Ohmsford had understood the meaning of the phrase since he was a boy. It meant that he would be shaped and reshaped by the events of his life, so that everything that happened would be in some way a consequence of what had gone before. It meant that the people he came to know would influence his conduct and his beliefs. It meant that his experiences of the past would impact his decisions of the future.

It meant that life was like a chain and the links that forged it could not be severed.

For Jair, the strongest of those links was to Garet Jax. That link, unlike any other, was a repository for memories he treasured so dearly that he protected them like glass ornaments, to be taken down from the shelf on which they were kept, polished, and then put away again with great care.

In the summer of the second year following his return from Graymark, he was still heavily under the influence of those memories. He woke often in the middle of the night from dreams of Garet Jax locked in battle with the Jachyra, heard echoes of the other's voice in conversations with his friends and neighbors, and caught sudden glimpses of the Weapons Master in the faces of strangers. He was not distressed by these occurrences; he was thrilled by them. They were an affirmation that he was keeping alive the past he cared so much about.

On the day the girl rode into Shady Vale, he was working at the family inn, helping the manager and his wife as a favor to his parents. He was standing on the porch, surveying the siding he had replaced after a windstorm had blown a branch through the wall. Something about the way she sat her horse caught his attention, drawing it away from his handiwork.

He shaded his eyes against the glare of the sun as it reflected off a metal roof when she turned out of the trees. She sat ramrod straight astride a huge black stallion with a white blaze on its forehead, her dark hair falling in a cascade of curls to her waist, thick and shining. She wasn't big, but she gave an immediate impression of possessing confidence that went beyond the need for physical strength.

She caught sight of him at the same time he saw her and turned the big black in his direction. She rode up to him and stopped, a mischievous smile appearing on her round, perky face as she brushed back loose strands of hair. "Cat got your tongue, Jair Ohmsford?"

"Kimber Boh," he said, not quite sure that it really was. "I don't believe it."

She swung down, dropped the reins in a manner that suggested this was all the black required, and walked over to give him a long, sustained hug. "You look all grown up," she said, and ruffled his curly blond hair to show she wasn't impressed.

He might have said the same about her. The feel of her body against his as she hugged him was a clear indication that she was beyond childhood. But it was difficult to accept. He still remembered the slender, tiny girl she had been two years ago when he had met her for the first time in the ruins of the Croagh in the aftermath of his battle to save Brin.

He shook his head. "I almost didn't recognize you."

She stepped back. "1 knew you right away." She looked around. "I always wanted to see where you lived. Is Brin here?"

She wasn't. Brin was living in the Highlands with Rone Leah, whom she had married in the spring. They were already expecting their first child; if it was a boy, they would name it Jair.

He shook his head. "No. She lives in Leah now. Why didn't you send word you were coming?"

"I didn't know myself until a little over a week ago." She glanced at the inn. "The ride has made me tired and thirsty. Why don't we go inside while we talk?"

They retreated to the cool interior of the inn and took a table at a window where the slant of the roof kept the sun off. The innkeeper brought over a pitcher of ale and two mugs, giving Jair a sly wink as he walked away.

"Does he give you a wink for every pretty girl you bring into this establishment?" Kimber asked when the innkeeper was out of earshot. "Are you a regular here?"

He blushed. "My parents own the inn. Kimber, what are you doing here?"

She considered the question. "I'm not entirely sure. I came to find you and to persuade you to come with me. But now that I'm here, I don't know that I have the words to do it. In fact, I might just not even try. I might just stay here and visit until you send me away. What would you say to that?"

He leaned back in his chair and smiled. "I guess I would say you were welcome to stay as long as you like. Is that what you want?"

She sipped at her ale and shook her head. "What I want doesn't matter. Maybe what you want doesn't matter either." She looked out the window into the sunshine. "Grandfather sent me. He said to tell you that what we thought we had finished two years ago isn't quite finished after all. There appears to be a loose thread that needs snipping off."

"A loose thread?"

She looked back at him. "Remember when your sister burned the book of the Ildatch at Graymark?"

He nodded. "I'm not likely to forget."

"Grandfather says she missed a page."

THEY ATE dinner at his home, a dinner that he prepared himself, which included soup made of fresh garden vegetables, bread, and a plate of cheeses and dried fruits stored for his use by his parents, who were south on a journey to places where their special healing talents were needed. They sat at the dinner table and watched the darkness descend in a slow curtain of shadows that draped the countryside like black silk. The sky stayed clear and the stars came out, brilliant and glittering against the firmament.

"He wouldn't tell you why he needs me?" Jair asked for what must have been the fifth or sixth time.

She shook her head patiently. "He just said you were the one to bring, not your sister, not your parents, not Rone Leah. Just you."

"And he didn't say anything about the Elfstones either? You're sure about that?"

She looked at him, a hint of irritation in her blue eyes. "Do you know that this is one of the best meals I have ever eaten? It really is. This soup is wonderful, and I want to know how to make it. But for now, I am

content just to eat it. Why don't you stop asking questions and enjoy it, too?"

He responded with a rueful grimace and sipped at the soup, staying quiet for a few mouthfuls while he mulled things over. He was having difficulty accepting what she was telling him, let alone agreeing to what she was asking. Two years earlier, the Ohmsford siblings had taken separate paths to reach the hiding place of the Ildatch, the book of dark magic that had spawned first the Warlock Lord and his Skull Bearers in the time of Shea and Flick Ohmsford and then the Mord Wraiths in their own time. The magic contained in the book was so powerful that the book had taken on a life of its own, become a spirit able to subvert and ultimately re-form beings of flesh and blood into monstrous undead creatures. It had done so repeatedly and would have kept on doing so had Brin and he not succeeded in destroying it.

Of course, it had almost destroyed Brin first. Possessed of the magic of the wishsong, of the power to create or destroy through use of music and words, Brin was a formidable opponent, but an attractive ally, as well. Perhaps she would have become the latter instead of the former had Jair not reached her in time to prevent it. But it was for that very purpose that the King of the Silver River had sent him to find her after she had left with Allanon, and so he had known in advance what was expected of him. His own magic was of a lesser kind, an ability to appear to change things without actually being able to do so, but in this one instance it had proved sufficient to do what was needed.

Which was why he was somewhat confused by Kimber's grandfather's insistence on summoning him now. Whatever the nature of the danger presented by the threat of an Ildatch reborn, he was the least well-equipped member of the family to deal with it. He was also doubtful of the man making the selection, having seen enough of the wild-eyed and unpredictable Cogline to know that he wasn't always rowing with all his oars in the water. Kimber might have confidence in him, but that didn't mean Jair should.

An even bigger concern was the old man's assertion that somehow the Ildatch hadn't been completely destroyed when Brin had gone to such lengths to make certain that it was. She had used her magic to burn it to ashes, the whole tome, each and every page. So how could it have survived in any form? How could Brin have been mistaken about something so crucial?

He knew that he wasn't going to find out unless he went with Kimber to see the old man and hear him out, but it was a long journey to Hearthstone, which lay deep in the Eastland, a draining commitment of time and energy. Especially if it turned out that the old man was mistaken.

So he asked his questions, hoping to learn something helpful, waiting for a revelation. But soon he had asked the old ones more times than was necessary and had run out of new ones.

"I know you think Grandfather is not altogether coherent about some things," Kimber said. "You know as much even from the short amount of time you spent with him two years ago, so I don't have to pretend. I know he can be difficult and unsteady. But I also know that he sees things other men don't, that he has resources denied to them. I can read a trail and track it, but he can read signs on the air itself. He can make things out of compounds and powders that no one else has known how to make since the destruction of the Old World. He's more than he seems."

"So you believe that I should go, that there's a chance he might be right about the Ildatch?" Jair leaned forward again, his meal forgotten. "Tell me the truth, Kimber."

INDOMITABLE

"I think you would be wise to pay attention to what he has to say." Her face was calm, but her eyes troubled. "I have my own doubts about Grandfather, but I saw the way he was when he told me to come find you. It wasn't something done on a whim. It was done after a great deal of thought. He would have come himself, but I wouldn't let him. He is too old and frail. Since I wouldn't let him make the journey, I had to make it myself. I guess that says something about how I view the matter."

She looked down at her food and pushed it away. "Let's clean up, and then we can sit outside."

They carried off the dishes, washed them, and put them away, and then went out onto the porch and sat together on a wooden bench that looked off toward the southwest. The night was warm and filled with smells of jasmine and evergreen, and somewhere off in the darkness a stream trickled. They sat without speaking for a while, listening to the silvery sound of the water. An owl flew by, its dark shape momentarily silhouetted by moonlight. From down in the village came the faint sound of laughter.

"It seems like a long time since we were at Graymark," she said quietly. "A long time since everything that happened two years ago."

Jair nodded, remembering. "I've thought often about you and your grandfather. I wondered how you were. I don't know why I worried, though. You were fine before Brin and Rone found you. You've probably been fine since. Do you still have the moor cat?"

"Whisper? Yes. He keeps us both safe from the things we can't keep safe from on our own." She paused. "But maybe we aren't as fine as you think, Jair. Things change. Both Grandfather and I are older. He needs me more; I need him less. Whisper goes away more often and comes back less frequently. The country is growing up around us. It isn't as wild as it once was. There is a Dwarven village not five miles away and Gnome tribes migrate from the Wolfsktaag to the Ravenshorn and back again all the time." She shrugged. "It isn't the same."

"What will you do when your grandfather is gone?"

She laughed softly. "That might never happen. He might live forever." She sighed, gesturing vaguely with one slender hand. "Sometimes, I think about moving away from Hearthstone, of living somewhere else. I admit I want to see something of the larger world."

"Would you come down into the Borderlands, maybe?" He looked over at her. "Would you come live here? You might like it."

She nodded. "I might."

She didn't say anything else, so he went back to looking into the darkness, thinking it over. He would like having her here. He liked talking to her. He guessed that over time they might turn out to be good friends.

"I need you to come back with me," she said suddenly, looking at him with unexpected intensity. "I might as well tell you so. It has more to do with me than with Grandfather. I am worn out by him. I hate admitting it because it makes me sound weak. But he grates on me the older and more difficult he gets. I don't know if this business about the Ildatch is real or not. But I don't think I can get to the truth of it alone. I'm being mostly selfish by coming here and asking you to come to Hearthstone with me. Grandfather is set on this happening. Just having you talk with him might make a difference."

Jair shook his head doubtfully. "I barely know him. I don't see what difference having me there would make to anything."

She hesitated, then exhaled sharply. "My grandfather was there to help your sister when she needed it, Jair. I am asking you to return the favor. I think he needs you, whether the danger from the Ildatch is real or not. What's bothering him is real enough. I want you to come back with me and help settle things."

He thought about it a long time, making himself do so even though he already knew what he was going to say. He was thinking of what Garet Jax would do.

"All right, I'll come," he said finally.

Because he knew that this is what the Weapons Master would have done in his place.

HE LEFT a letter with the innkeeper for his parents, explaining where he was going, packed some clothes, and closed up the house. He already knew he would be in trouble when he returned, but that wasn't enough to keep him from going. The innkeeper loaned him a horse, a steady, reliable bay that could be depended on not to do anything unexpected or foolish. Jair was not much for horses, but he understood the need for one here, where there was so much distance to cover.

It took them a week to get to Hearthstone, riding north out of Shady Vale and the Duln Forests, around the western end of the Rainbow Lake, then up through Callahorn along the Mermidon River to the Rabb Plains. They crossed the Rabb, following its river into the Upper Anar, then rode down through the gap between the Wolfsktaag Mountains and Darklin Reach, threading the needle of the corridor between, staying safely back from the edges of both. As they rode, Jair found himself pondering how different the circumstances were now from the last time he had come into the Eastland. Then, he had been hunted at every turn, threatened by more dangers than he cared to remember. It had been Garet Jax who had saved his life time and again. Now he traveled without fear of attack, without having to look over his shoulder, and Garet Jax was only a memory.

"Do you think we might have lived other lives before this one?" Kimber asked him on their last night out before reaching Hearthstone.

They were sitting in front of a fire in a grove of trees flanking the south branch of the Rabb, deep within the forests of Darklin Reach. The horses grazed contentedly a short distance off, and moonlight flooded the grassy flats that stretched away about them. There was a hint of a chill in the air this night, a warning of autumn's approach.

Jair smiled. "I don't think about it at all. I have enough trouble living the life I have without wondering if there were others."

"Or if there will be others after this one?" She brushed at her long hair, which she kept tied back as they rode, but let down at night in a tumbled mass. "Grandfather thinks so. I guess I do, too. I think everything is connected. Lives, like moments in time, are all linked together, fish in a stream, swimming and swimming. The past coming forward to become the future."

He looked off into the dark. "I think we are connected to the past, but mostly to the events and the people that shaped it. I think we are always reaching back in some way, bringing forward what we remember, sometimes for information, sometimes just for comfort. I don't remember other lives, but I remember the past of this one. I remember the people who were in it."

She waited a moment, then moved over to sit beside him. "The way you said that—are you thinking about what happened two years ago at Heaven's Well?"

He shrugged.

"About the one you called the Weapons Master?"

He stared at her. "How did you know that?"

"It isn't much of a mystery, Jair. You talked about no one else afterward. Only him, the one who saved you on the Croagh, the one who fought the Jachyra. Don't you remember?"

He nodded. "I guess."

"Maybe your connection with him goes farther back in time than just this life." She lifted an eyebrow at him. "Have you thought about that? Maybe you were joined in another life as well, and that's why he made such an impression on you."

Jair laughed. "I think he made an impression on me because he was the best fighter I have ever seen. He was so…" He stopped himself, searching for the right word. "Indomitable." His smile faded. "Nothing could stand against him, not even a Jachyra. Not even something that was too much for Allanon."

"But I might still be right about past lives," she persisted. She put her hand on his shoulder and squeezed. "You can grant me that much, can't you, Valeman?"

He could, that and much more. He wanted to tell her so, but didn't know how without sounding foolish. He was attracted to her, and it surprised him. Having thought of her for so long as a little girl, he was having trouble accepting that she was now full grown. Such a transition didn't seem possible. It confused his thinking, the past conflicting with the present. How did she feel about him, as changed in his own way as she was in hers? He wondered, but could not make himself ask.

In late afternoon of the following day, they reached Hearthstone. He had never been here before, but he had heard Brin describe the chimney-shaped rock so often that he knew at once what it was. He caught sight of it as they rode through the trees, a dark pinnacle overlooking a shallow, wooded valley. Its distinctive, rugged formation seemed right for this country, a land of dark rumors and strange happenings. Yet that was in the past, as well. Things were different now. They had come in on a road, where two years before there had been no roads. They had passed the newly settled Dwarf village and seen the houses and heard the voices of children. The country was growing up, the wilderness pushed back. Change was the one constant in an ever-evolving world.

They reached the cottage shortly afterward. It was constructed of wood and timber with porches front and back, its walls grown thick with ivy and the grounds surrounding it planted with gardens and ringed with walkways and bushes. It had a well-cared-for look to it; everything was neatly planted and trimmed, a mix of colors and forms that were pleasing to the eye. It didn't look so much like a wilderness cottage as a village home. Behind the house, a paddock housed a mare and a foal. A milk cow was grazing there as well. Sheds lined the back of the paddock, neatly painted. Shade trees helped conceal the buildings from view; Jair hadn't caught even a glimpse of roofs on the ride in.

He glanced over at her. "Do you look after all this by yourself?"

"Mostly." She gave him a wry smile. "I like looking after a home. I always have, ever since I was old enough to help do so."

They rode into the yard and dismounted, and instantly Cogline appeared through the doorway. He was ancient and stick-thin beneath his baggy clothing, and his white hair stuck out in all directions, as if he might have just come awake. He pulled at his beard as he came up to them, his fingers raking the wiry hairs. His eyes were sharp and questioning, and he was already scanning Jair as if not quite sure what to make of him.

"So!" He approached with that single word and stood so close that the Valeman was forced to take a step back. He peered intently into Jair's blue eyes, took careful note of his Elven features. "Is this him?"

"Yes, Grandfather." Kimber sounded embarrassed.

"You're certain? No mistake?"

"Yes, Grandfather."

"Because he could be someone else, you know. He could be *anybody* else!" Cogline furrowed his already deeply lined brow. "Are you young Ohmsford? The boy, Jair?"

Jair nodded. "I am. Don't you remember me? We met two years ago in the ruins of Graymark."

The old man stared at him as if he hadn't heard the question. Jair could feel the other's hard gaze probing in a way that was not altogether pleasant. "Is this necessary?" he asked finally. "Can't we go inside and sit down?"

"When I say so!" the other replied. "When I say I am finished! Don't interrupt my study!"

"Grandfather!" Kimber exclaimed.

The old man ignored her. "Let me see your hands," he said.

Jair held out his hands, palms up. Cogline studied them carefully for a moment, grunted as if he had found whatever it was he was looking for, and said, "Come inside, and I'll fix you something to eat."

They went into the cottage and seated themselves at the rough-hewn wooden dining table, but it was Kimber who ended up preparing a stew for them to eat. While she did so, directing admonitions at her grandfather when she thought them necessary, Cogline rambled on about the past and Jair's part in it, a bewildering hodge-podge of information and observation.

"I remember you," he said. "Just a boy, coming out of Graymark's ruins with your sister, the two of you covered in dust and smelling of death! Hah! I know something of that smell, I can tell you! Fought many a monster come out of the netherworld, long before you were born, before any who live now were born and a good deal more who are long dead. Might have left the order, but didn't lose the skills. Not a one. Never listened to me, any of them, but that didn't make me give up. The new mirrors the old. You can't disconnect science and magic. They're all of a piece, and the lessons of one are the lessons of the other. Allanon knew as much. Knew just enough to get himself killed."

Jair had no idea what he was talking about, but perked up on hearing the Druid's name. "You knew Allanon?"

"Not when he was alive. Know him now that he's dead, though. Your sister, she was a gift to him. She was the answer to what he needed when he saw the end coming. It's like that for some, the gift. Maybe for you, too, one day."

"What gift?"

"You know, I was a boy once. I was a Druid once, too."

Jair stared at him, not quite knowing whether to accept this or not. It was hard to think of him as a boy, but thinking of him as a Druid was harder still. If the old man really was a Druid—not that Jair thought for a moment that he was—what was he doing here, out in the wilderness, living with Kimber? "I thought Allanon was the last of the Druids," he said.

The old man snorted. "You thought a lot of things that weren't so." He shoved back his plate of stew, having hardly touched it. "Do you want to know what you're doing here?"

Jair stopped eating in mid-bite. Kimber, sitting across from him, blinked once and said, "Maybe you should wait until he's finished dinner, Grandfather."

The old man ignored her. "Your sister thought the Ildatch destroyed," he said. "She was wrong. Wasn't her fault, but she was wrong. She burned it to ash, turned it to a charred ruin and that should have been the end of it, but it wasn't. You want to sit outside while we have this discussion? The open air and the night sky make it easier to think things through sometimes."

They went outside onto the front porch, where the sky west was turning a brilliant mix of purple and rose above the treetops and the sky east already boasted a partial moon and a scattering of stars. The old man took possession of the only rocker, and Jair and Kimber sat together on a high-backed wooden bench. It occurred to the Valeman that he needed to rub down and feed his horse, a task he would have completed by now if he had been thinking straight.

The old man rocked in silence for a time, then gestured abruptly at Jair. "Last month, on a night when the moon was full and the sky a sea of stars, beautiful night, I woke and walked down to the little pond that lies just south. I don't know why, I just did. Something made me. I lay in the grass and slept, and while I slept, I had a dream. Only it was more a vision than a dream. I used to have such visions often. I was closer to the shades of the dead then, and they would come to me because I was receptive to their needs.

But that was long ago, and I had thought such things at an end."

He seemed to reflect on the idea for a moment, lost in thought. "I was a Druid then."

"Grandfather," Kimber prodded softly.

The old man looked back at Jair. "In my dream, Allanon's shade came to me out of the netherworld. It spoke to me. It told me that the Ildatch was not yet destroyed, that a piece of it still survived. One page only, seared at the edges, shaken loose and blown beneath the stones of the keep in the fiery destruction of the rest. Perhaps the book found a way to save that one page in its death throes. I don't know. The shade didn't tell me. Only that it had survived your sister's efforts and been found in the rubble by Mwellrets who sought artifacts that would lend them the power that had belonged to the Mord Wraiths. Those rets knew what they had because the page told them, a whisper that promised great things! It had life, even as a fragment, so powerful was its magic!"

Jair glanced at Kimber, who blinked at him uncertainly. Clearly, this was news to her as well. "One page," he said to the old man, "isn't enough to be dangerous, is it? Unless there is a spell the Mwellrets can make use of?"

Cogline ran his hand through his wiry thatch of white hair. "Not enough? Yes, that was my thought, too. One page, out of so many. What harm? I dismissed the vision on waking, convinced it was a malignant intrusion on a peaceful life, a groundless fear given a momentary foothold by an old man's frailness. But it came again, a second time, this time while I slept in my own bed. It was stronger than before, more insistent. The shade chided me for my indecision, for my failings past and present. It told me to find you and bring you here. It gave me no peace, not that night or after."

He looked genuinely distressed now, as if the memory of the shade's visit was a haunting of the sort he wished he had never encountered. Jair understood better now why Kimber felt it so important to summon him. Cogline was an old man teetering on the brink of emotional collapse. He might be hallucinating or he might have connected with the shades of the dead, Allanon or not, but whatever he had experienced, it had left him badly shaken.

"Now that I am here, what am I expected to do?" he asked.

The old man looked at him. There was a profound sadness mirrored in his ancient eyes. "I don't know," he said. "I wasn't told."

Then he looked off into the darkness and didn't speak again.

"I'M SORRY about this," Kimber declared later. There was a pronounced weariness in her voice. "I didn't think he was going to be this vague once he had the chance to speak with you. I should have known better. I shouldn't have brought you."

They were sitting together on the bench again, sipping at mugs of cold ale and listening to the night. They had put the old man to sleep a short while earlier, tucking him into his bed and sitting with him until he began to snore. Kimber had done her best to hasten the process with a cup of medicated tea.

He smiled at her. "Don't be sorry. I'm glad you brought me. I don't know if I can help, but I think you were right about not wanting to handle this business alone. I can see where he could become increasingly more difficult if you tried to put him off."

"But it's all such a bunch of nonsense! He hasn't been out of his bed in months. He hasn't slept down by the pond. Whatever dreams he's been having are the result of his refusal to eat right." She blew out a sharp breath in frustration. "All this business about the Ildatch surviving somehow in a page fragment! I used to believe everything he told me, when I was little and still thought him the wisest man in the world. But now I think that he's losing his mind."

Jair sipped at his ale. "I don't know. He seems pretty convinced."

She stared at him. "You don't believe him, do you?"

"Not entirely. But it might be he's discovered something worth paying attention to. Dreams have a way of revealing things we don't understand right away. They take time to decipher. But once we've thought about it..."

"Why would Allanon's shade come to Grandfather in a dream and ask him to bring you here rather than just appearing to you?" she interrupted heatedly. "What sense does it make to go through Grandfather? He would not be high on the list of people you might listen to!"

"There must be a reason, if he's really had a vision from a shade. He must be involved in some important way."

He looked at her for confirmation, but she had turned away, her mouth compressed in a tight, disapproving line. "Are you going to help him, Jair? Are you going to try to make him see that he is imagining things or are you going to feed this destructive behavior with pointless encouragement?"

He flushed at the rebuke, but kept his temper. Kimber was looking to him to help her grandfather find a way out of the quicksand of his delusions, and instead of doing so, he was offering to jump in himself. But he couldn't dismiss the old man's words as easily as she could. He was not burdened by years and experiences shared; he did not see Cogline in the same way she did. Nor was he so quick to disbelieve visions and dreams and shades. He had encountered more than a few himself, not the least of which was the visit from the King of the Silver River, two years earlier, under similar circumstances. If not for that visit, a visit he might have dismissed if he had been less open-minded, Brin would have been lost to him and the entire world changed. It was not something you forgot easily. Not wanting to believe was not always the best approach to things you didn't understand.

"Kimber," he said quietly, "I don't know yet what I am going to do. I don't know enough to make a decision. But if I dismiss your grandfather's words out of hand, it might be worse than if I try to see through them to what lies beneath."

He waited while she looked off into the distance, her eyes still hot and her mouth set. Then finally, she turned back to him, nodding slowly. "I'm sorry. I didn't mean to attack you. You were good enough to come when I asked, and I am letting my frustration get in the way of my good sense. I know you mean to help."

"I do," he reassured her. "Let him sleep through the night, and then see if he's had the vision again. We can talk about it when he wakes and is fresh. We might be able to discover its source."

She shook her head quickly. "But what if it's real, Jair? What if it's true? What if I've brought you here for selfish reasons and I've placed you in real danger? I didn't mean for that to happen, but what if it does?"

She looked like a child again, waiflike and lost. He smiled and cocked one Elfish eyebrow at her. "A moment ago, you were telling me there wasn't a chance it was real. Are you ready to abandon that ground just because I said we shouldn't dismiss it out of hand? I didn't say I believed it either. I just said there might be some truth to it."

"I don't want there to be any. I want it to be Grandfather's wild imagination at work and nothing more." She stared at him intently. "I want this all to go away, far away, and not come back again. We've had enough of Mord Wraiths and books of dark magic."

He nodded slowly, then reached out and touched her lightly on the cheek, surprising himself with his boldness. When she closed her eyes, he felt his face grow hot and quickly took his hand away. He felt suddenly dizzy. "Let's wait and see, Kimber," he said. "Maybe the dream won't come to him again."

She opened her eyes. "Maybe," she whispered.

He turned back toward the darkness, took a long, cool swallow of his ale, and waited for his head to clear.

THE DREAM didn't come to Cogline that night, after all. Instead, it came to Jair Ohmsford.

He was not expecting it when he crawled into his bed, weary from the long journey and slightly muddled from a few too many cups of ale. The horses were rubbed down and fed, his possessions were put away in the cupboard and the cottage was dark. He didn't know how long he slept before it began, only that it happened all at once, and when it did, it was as if he were completely awake and alert.

He stood at the edge of a vast body of water that stretched away as far as the eye could see, its surface gray and smooth, reflecting a sky as flat and color-less as itself, so that there was no distinction between the one and the other. The shade was already there, hovering above its surface, a huge dark specter that dwarfed him in size and blotted out a whole section of the horizon behind it. Its hood concealed its features, and all that was visible were pinpricks of red light like eyes burning out of a black hole.

—Do you know me—

He did, of course. He knew instinctively, without having to think about it, without having been given more than those four words with which to work. "You are Allanon."

—In life. In death, his shade. Do you remember me as I was—

Jair saw the Druid once again, waiting for Brin and Rone Leah and himself as they returned home late at night, a dark and imposing figure, too large somehow for their home. He heard the Druid speak to them of the Ildatch and the Mord Wraiths. The

strong features and the determined voice mesmerized him. He had never known anyone as dominating as Allanon—except, perhaps, for Garet Jax.

"I remember you," he said.

—Watch—

An image appeared on the air before him, gloomy and indistinct. It revealed the ruins of a vast fortress, mounds of rubble against a backdrop of forest and mountains. Graymark destroyed. Shadowy figures moved through the rubble, poking amid the broken stones. Bearing torches, a handful went deep inside, down tunnels in danger of collapse. They were cloaked and hooded, but the flicker of light on their hands and faces revealed patches of reptilian scales. Mwellrets. They wound their way deeper into the ruins, into fresh-made catacombs, into places where only darkness and death could be found. They proceeded slowly, taking their time, pausing often to search nooks and crannies, each hollow in the earth that might offer concealment.

Then one of the Mwellrets began to dig, an almost frantic effort, pulling aside stones and timbers, hissing like a snake. It labored for long minutes, all alone, the others gone elsewhere. Dust and blood soon coated its scaly hide, and its breath came in gasps that suggested near-exhaustion.

But in the end, it found what it sought, pulling free from the debris a seared, torn page of a book, a page with writing on it that pulsed like veins beneath skin…

—Watch—

A second image appeared, this one of another fortress, one he didn't recognize right away, even though it seemed familiar. It was as dark and brooding as Graymark had been, as thick with shadows and gloom, as hard-edged and rough-hewn. The image lingered only a moment on the outer walls, then took the Valeman deep inside, past gates and battlements and into the nether regions. In a room dimly lit by torches that smoked and steamed in damp, stale air, a cluster of Mwellrets hovered over the solitary book page retrieved from Graymark's ruins.

They were engaged in an arcane rite. Jair could not be certain, but he had the distinct feeling that they were not entirely aware of what was happening to them. They were moving in concert, like gears in a machine, each one in sync with the others. They kept their heads lowered and their eyes fixed, and there was a hypnotic sound to their voices and movements that suggested they were responding to something he couldn't see. In the gloom and smoke, they reminded him of the Spider Gnomes on Toffer Ridge, come to make sacrifice of themselves to the Werebeasts, come to give up the lives of a few in the mistaken belief that it was for the good of the many.

As one, they moved their palms across the surface of the paper, taking in the feel of the veined writing, murmuring furtive chants and small prayers. Beneath their reptilian fingers, the page glowed and the writing pulsed. It was responding to their efforts. Jair could feel the raw pull of a siphoning, a leaching away of life.

The remnant of the Ildatch, in search of a way back from the edge of extinction, in need of nourishment that would enable it to recall and put to use the spells it had lost, was feeding.

The image faded. He was alone again with Allanon's shade, two solitary figures facing each other across an empty vista. The gloom had grown thicker and the sky darker. The lake no longer reflected light of any sort.

In the aftermath of the visions, he had realized why the second fortress had seemed so familiar. It was Dun Fee Aran, the Gnome prisons where he had been taken by the Mwellret Stythys to be coerced into giving up his magic and eventually his life. He remembered his despair on being cast into the cell allotted to him, deep beneath the earth in the bowels of the keep, alone in the darkness and silence. He remembered his fear.

"I can't go back there," he whispered, already anticipating what the shade was going to ask of him.

But the shade asked nothing of him. Instead, it gestured and for a third and final time, the air before the Valeman began to shimmer.

—Watch—

"I KNEW it!" Cogline exclaimed gleefully. "It's still alive! Didn't I tell you so? Wasn't that just what I said? You thought me a crazy old man, Granddaughter, but how crazy do I look to you now? Hallucinations? Wild imaginings? Hah! Am I still to be treated as if I were a delicate flower? Am I still to be humored and coddled?"

He began dancing about the room and cackling like the madman that, Jair guessed, he was as close as possible to being while still marginally sane. The Valeman watched him patiently, trying not to look at

Kimber, who was so angry and disgusted that he could feel the heat radiating from her glare. It was morning now, and they sat across from each other at the old wooden dining table, bathed in bright splashes of sunlight that streamed through the open windows and belied the darkness of the moment.

"You haven't told us yet what the shade expects of you," Kimber said quietly, though he could not mistake the edge to her words.

"What you have already guessed," he answered, meeting her gaze reluctantly. "What I knew even before the third image showed it to me. I have to go to Dun Fee Aran and put a stop to what's happening."

Cogline stopped dancing. "Well, you can do that, I expect," he said, shrugging aside the implications. "You did it once before, didn't you?"

"No, Grandfather, he did not," Kimber corrected him impatiently. "That was his sister, and I don't understand why she wasn't sent for, if the whole idea is to finish the job she started two years ago. It's her fault the Ildatch is still alive."

Jair shook his head. "It isn't anybody's fault. It just happened. In any case, Brin's married and pregnant and doesn't use the magic anymore."

Nor would she ever use it again, he was thinking. It had taken her a long time to get over what happened to her at the Maelmord. He had seen how long it had taken. He didn't know that she had ever been the same since. She had warned him that the magic was dangerous, that you couldn't trust it, that it could turn on you even when you thought it was your friend. He remembered the haunted look in her eyes.

He leaned forward, folding his hands in front of him. "Allanon's shade made it clear that she can't be exposed to the Ildatch a second time—not even to a fragment of a page. She is too vulnerable to its magic, too susceptible to what it can do to humans, even one as powerful as she is. Someone else has to go, someone, who hasn't been exposed to the power of the book before."

Kimber reached out impulsively and took hold of his hands. "But why you, Jair? Others could do this."

"Maybe not. Dun Fee Aran is a Mwellret stronghold, and the page is concealed somewhere deep inside. Just finding it presents problems that would stop most from even getting close. But I have the magic of the wishsong, and I can use it to disguise myself. I can make it appear as if I'm not there. That way, I can gain sufficient time to find the page without being discovered."

"The boy is right!" Cogline exclaimed, animated anew by the idea. "He is the perfect choice!"

"Grandfather!" Kimber snapped at him.

The old man turned, running his gnarled fingers through his tangled beard. "Stop yelling at me!"

"Then stop jumping to ridiculous conclusions! Jair is not the perfect choice. He might be able to get past the rets and into the fortress, but then he has to destroy the page and get out again. How is he to do that when all his magic can do is create illusions? Smoke and mirrors! How is he to defend himself against a real attack, one he is almost sure to come up against at some point?"

"We'll go with him!" the old man declared. "We'll be his protectors! We'll take Whisper—just as soon as he comes back from wherever he's wandered off to. Dratted cat!"

Kimber ran a hand across her eyes as if trying to see things more clearly. "Jair, do you understand what I am saying? This is hopeless!"

The Valeman didn't answer right away. He was remembering the third vision shown him by Allanon's shade, the one he hadn't talked about. A jumble of uncertain images clouded by shadowy movement and wildness, it had frightened and confused him. Yet it had imbued him with a certainty of success, as well, a certainty so strong and unmistakable that he could not dismiss it.

"The shade said that I would find a way," he answered her. He hesitated. "If I just believe in myself."

She stared at him. "If you just believe in yourself?"

"I know. It sounds foolish. And I'm terrified of Dun Fee Aran, have been since I was imprisoned there by the Mwellret Stythys two years ago on my way to find Brin. I thought I was going to die in those cells. And maybe worse was going to happen first. I have never been so afraid of anything. I swore, once I was out of there, that I would never go back, not for any reason."

He took a deep breath and exhaled slowly. "But I think that I have to go back anyway, in part because it's necessary if the Ildatch is to be stopped, but also because Allanon made me feel that I shouldn't be afraid any more. He gave me a sense of reassurance that this wouldn't be like the last time, that it would be different because I am older and stronger now—better able to face what's waiting there."

"Telling you all this might just be a way to get you to do what he wants," Kimber pointed out. "It might be a Druid trick, a deception of the sort that shades are famous for."

He nodded. "It might. But it doesn't feel that way. It doesn't feel false. It feels true."

"Of course, it would," she said quietly. She looked miserable. "I brought you here to help Grandfather find peace of mind with his dreams, not to risk your life because of them. Everything I told you I was afraid was going to happen is happening. I hate it."

She was squeezing his hands so hard she was hurting him. "If I didn't come, Kimber," he said, "who would act on your grandfather's dreams? It isn't something we planned, either of us, but we can't ignore what's needed. I have to go. I have to."

She nodded slowly, her hands withdrawing from his. "I know." She looked at Cogline, who was standing very still now, looking distressed, as if suddenly aware of what he had brought about. She smiled gently at him. "I know, Grandfather."

The old man nodded slowly, but the joy had gone out of him.

INDOMITABLE

IT WAS decided they would set out the following day. It was a journey of some distance, even if they went on horseback. It would take them the better part of a week to get through the Ravenshorn Mountains and skirt the edges of Olden Moor to where Dun Fee Aran looked out over the Silver River in the shadow of the High Bens. This was rugged country, most of it still wilderness, beyond the spread of Dwarf settlements and Gnome camps. Much of it was swamp and jungle, and some of it was too dangerous to try to pass through. A direct line of approach was out of the question. At best, they would be able to find a path along the eastern edge of the Ravenshorn. They would have to carry their own supplies and water. They would have to go prepared for the worst.

Jair was not pleased with the thought that both Kimber and Cogline would be going with him, but there was nothing he could do about that, either. He was going back into country that had been unfamiliar to him two years earlier and was unfamiliar to him now. He wouldn't be able to find his way without help, and the only help at hand was the girl and her grandfather, both of whom knew the Anar much better than anyone else he would have been able to turn to. It would have been nice to leave them behind in safety, but he doubted that they would have permitted it even if he hadn't had need of them. For reasons that were abundantly apparent, they intended to see this matter through with him.

They spent the remainder of the day putting together supplies, a process that was tedious and somehow emotionally draining, as if the act of preparation was tantamount to climbing to a cliff ledge before jumping off. There wasn't much conversation exchanged, and most of what was said concerned the task itself. That the effort helped pass the time was the best that could be said for it.

More often than he cared to admit, Jair found himself wondering how far he was pressing his luck by going back into country he had been fortunate to escape from once already. He might argue that this time, like the last, he was going because he had no choice, but in fact he did. He could walk away from the dreams and their implications. He could argue that Kimber was right and that he was being used for reasons that he did not appreciate. He could even argue that efforts at reviving the Ildatch were doomed in any case, its destruction by his sister's magic so complete that trying to re-create the book from a single page was impossible. He could stop everything they were doing simply by announcing that he was going home to ask help from his parents and sister. It would be wiser to involve them in any case, wouldn't it?

But he would not do that. He knew he wouldn't even as he was telling himself he could. He was just new enough at being grown up not to want to ask for help unless he absolutely had to. It diminished him in his own mind, if not in fact, to seek assistance from his family. It was almost as if they expected it of him, the youngest and least experienced, the one they all had been helping for so long. There was an admission of failure written into such an act, one that he could not abide. This was something he could do, after all. He had gone into this country once, and dangerous or not, he could go into it again.

His mood did not improve with the coming of nightfall and the realization that there was nothing else to be done but to wait for morning. They ate the dinner Kimber made them, the old man filling the silence with thoughts of the old days and the new world, of

Druids past and a future without them. There would be a time when they would return, he insisted. The Druids would be needed again, you could depend on it. Jair kept his mouth shut. He did not want to say what he was thinking about Druids and the need for them.

He dreamed again that night, but not of the shade of Allanon. In his dream, he was already down inside the fortress at Dun Fee Aran, working his way along corridors shrouded in damp and gloom, hopelessly lost and searching for a way out. A sibilant voice whose source he could not divine whispered in his ear, *Never leavess thiss plasse.* Terrifying creatures besieged him but he could see nothing of them but their shadows. The longer he wandered, the greater his sense of foreboding, until finally it was all he could do to keep from screaming.

When a room opened before him, its interior as black as ink, he stopped at the threshold, afraid to go farther, knowing that if he did so, something terrible would happen. But he could not help himself because the shadows were closing in from behind, pressing up against him, and soon they would smother him completely. So he stepped forward into the room—one step, two, three—feeling his way with a caution he prayed might save him and yet feared wouldn't.

INDOMITABLE

Then a hand stretched toward him, slender and brown, and he knew it was Kimber's. He was reaching for it, so grateful he wanted to cry, when something shoved him hard from behind and he tumbled forward into a pit. He began to fall, unable to save himself, the hand that had reached for him gone, his efforts at escape doomed. He kept falling, waiting for the impact that would shatter his bones and leave him lifeless, knowing it was getting closer, closer...

Then a second hand reached out to catch hold of him in a grip so powerful it defied belief, and the falling stopped...

He woke with a start, jerking upright in bed, gasping for breath and clutching at the blanket he had kicked aside in his thrashings. It took him a moment to get out of the dream completely, to regain control of his emotions so that he no longer feared he might begin to fall again. He swung his legs over the side of the bed and sat with his head between his knees, taking long, slow breaths. The dream had made him feel frightened and alone.

Finally, he looked up. Outside, the first patch of dawn's brightness was visible above the trees. Sudden panic rushed through him.

What was he doing?

He knew in that moment that he wasn't equal to the task he had set himself. He wasn't strong or brave enough. He didn't possess the necessary skills or experience. He hadn't lived even two decades. He might be considered a man in some quarters, but in the place that counted, in his heart, he was still a boy. If he were smart, he would slip out the door now and ride back the way he had come. He would give up on this business and save his life.

He considered doing so for long moments, knowing he should act on his instincts, knowing as well that he couldn't.

Outside, the sky continued to brighten slowly into day. He stood, finally, and began to dress.

THEY DEPARTED at midmorning, riding their horses north out of Hearthstone toward the passes below Toffer Ridge that would take them through the Ravenshorn and into the deep Eastland. A voluble Cogline led the way, having mapped out a route that would allow them to travel on horseback all the way to Dun Fee Aran barring unforeseen weather or circumstances, a fact that he insisted on repeating at every opportunity. Admittedly, the old man knew the country better than anyone save the nomadic Gnome tribes and a few local Trackers. What worried Jair was how well he would remember what he knew when it counted. But there was nothing he could do about Cogline's unpredictability; all he could do was hope for the best. At present, the old man seemed fine, even eager to get on with things, which was as much as Jair could expect.

He was also upset that Whisper had failed to reappear before their departure, for the moor cat would have been a welcome addition to their company. Few living creatures, man or beast, would dare to challenge a full-grown moor cat. But there was no help for this, either. They would have to get along without him.

The weather stayed good for the first three days, and travel was uneventful. They rode north to the passes that crossed down over Toffer Ridge, staying well below Olden Moor, where the Werebeasts lived, traveling by daylight to make certain of their path. Each night, they would camp in a spot carefully chosen by Cogline and approved by Kimber, a place where they could keep watch and be reasonably certain of their safety. Each night, Kimber would prepare a meal for them and then put her grandfather to bed. Each night, the old man went without complaining and fell instantly asleep.

"It's the tea," she confided in Jair. "I put a little of his medication in it to quiet him down, the same medication I used at Hearthstone. Sometimes, it is the only way he can sleep."

They encountered few other travelers, and there was an ordinariness to their journey that belied its nature. At times it felt to Jair as if he might be on nothing more challenging than a wilderness outing, an exploration of unfamiliar country with no other purpose than to have a look around. At such times, it was difficult to think about what was waiting at the end. The end seemed far away and unrelated to the present, as if it might belong to another experience altogether.

But those moments of complacency never lasted, and when they dissipated he reverted to a dark consideration of the particulars of what would be required when he arrived at Dun Fee Aran. His conclusions were always the same. Getting inside would be easy enough. He knew how he would use his magic to disguise himself, how he would employ it to stay hidden. Unlike Brin, he had never stopped using it, practicing constantly, testing its limits. So long as he remembered not to press himself beyond those limits, he would be all right.

It was being caught out and exposed once he was inside that concerned him. He did not intend for this to happen, but if it did, what would he do? He was older and stronger than he had been two years ago, and he had studied weapons usage and self-defense since his return to the Vale. But he was not a practiced fighter, and he would be deep in the center of an enemy stronghold. That his sole allies were a young woman and a half-crazed old man was not reassuring. Kimber carried those throwing knives with which she was so lethal, and the old man his bag of strange powders and chemicals, some of which could bring down entire walls, but Jair was not inclined to rely on either. When he wasn't thinking about turning around and going home—which he found himself doing at least once a day—he was thinking about how he could persuade Kimber and her grandfather not to go with him into Dun Fee Aran. Whatever his own fate, he did not want harm to come to them. He was the one who had been summoned and dispatched by Allanon's shade. The task of destroying the Ildatch fragment had been given to him.

His fears and doubts haunted him. They clung to him like the dust of the road, tiny reminders that this business was not going to end well, that he was not equal to the task he had been given. He could not shake them, could not persuade himself that their insistent little voices were lies designed to erode his already paper-thin confidence. With every mile traveled, he felt more and more the boy he had been when he had come this way before. Dun Fee Aran was a fire pit of terror and the Mwellrets were the monsters that stirred its coals. He found himself wishing he had his companions from before—Garet Jax, the Borderman Helt, the Elven Prince Edain Elessedil, and the Dwarf Foraker. Even the taciturn, disgruntled Gnome Slanter would have been welcome. But except for the Gnome, whom he had not seen since their parting two years earlier, they had all died at Graymark. There was no possibility of replacing them, of finding allies of the same mettle. If he was determined not to involve Cogline and Kimber as more than guides and traveling companions, he would have to go it alone.

INDOMITABLE

On the fourth day, the weather turned stormy. At dawn, a dark wall of clouds rolled in from the west, and by midmorning it was raining heavily. By now they were through the Ravenshorn and riding southeast in the shadow of the mountains. The terrain was rocky and brush-clogged, and they were forced to dismount and walk their horses through the increasingly heavy downpour. Cloaked and hooded, they were effectively shut away from one another, each become a shadowy, faceless form hunched against the rain.

Locked away in the cold dampness of his water-soaked coverings, Jair found himself thinking incongruously that he had underestimated his chances of succeeding, that he was better prepared than he had thought earlier, that his magic would see him through. All he had to do was get inside Dun Fee Aran, wait for his chance, and destroy the Ildatch remnant. It wasn't like the last time, when the book of magic was a sentient being, able to protect itself. There weren't any Mord Wraiths to avoid. The Mwellrets were dangerous, but not in the same way as the walkers. He could do this. He could manage it.

He believed as much for about two hours, and then the doubts and fears returned, and his confidence evaporated. Slogging through the murk and mud, he saw himself walking a path to a cliff edge, taking a road that could only end one way.

His dark mood returned, and the weight of his inadequacies descended anew.

THAT NIGHT they made camp below Graymark on the banks of the Silver River, settled well back in the concealment of the hardwoods. They built a fire in the shelter of oaks grown so thick that their limbs blocked away all but small patches of the sky. Deadwood was plentiful, some of it dry enough to burn even after the downpour. Closer to Dun Fee Aran and the Mwellrets, they might have chosen not to risk it, but the most dangerous creatures abroad in these woods were of the four-legged variety. This far out in the wilderness, they were unlikely to encounter anything else.

Still, not long after they had cooked and eaten their dinner, they were startled by a clanking sound and the sharp bray of a pack animal. Then a voice called to them from the darkness, asking for permission to come in. Cogline gave it, grumbling under his breath as he did so, and their visitor walked into the firelight leading a mule on a rope halter. The man was tall and thin, cloaked head to foot in an old greatcoat that had seen hard use. The mule was a sturdy-looking animal bearing a wooden rack from which hung dozens of pots and pans and cooking implements. A peddler and his wares had stumbled on them.

The man tethered his mule and sat down at the fire, declining the cup of tea that was offered in favor of one filled with ale, which he gulped down gratefully. "Long, wet day," he declared in a weary voice. "This helps put it right."

They gave him what food was left over, still warm in the cooking pot, and watched him eat. "This is good," he announced, nodding in Kimber's direction. "First hot meal in a while and likely to be the last. Don't see many campfires out this way. Don't see many people, for that matter. But I'm more than ready to share company this night. Hope you don't mind."

"What are you doing way out here?" Jair asked him, taking advantage of the opening he had offered.

The peddler paused in mid-bite and gave him a wry smile. "I travel this way several times a year, servicing the places other peddlers won't. Might not look like it, but there are villages at the foot of the mountains that need what I sell. I pass through, do my business, and go home again, out by the Rabb. It's a lot of traveling, but I like it. I've only got me and my mule to worry about."

He finished putting the suspended bite into his mouth, chewed it carefully, and then said, "What about you? What brings you to the east side of the Ravenshorn? Pardon me for saying so, but you don't look like you belong here."

Jair exchanged a quick glance with Kimber. "Traveling up to Dun Fee Aran," Cogline announced before they could stop him. "Got some business ourselves. With the rets."

The peddler made a face. "I'd think twice about doing business with them." His tone of voice made clear his disgust. "Dun Fee Aran's no place for you. Get someone else to do your business, someone a little less…"

He trailed off, looking from one face to the next, clearly unable to find the words that would express his concern that a boy, a girl, and an old man would even think of trying to do business with Mwellrets.

"It won't take long," Jair said, trying to put a better face on the idea. "We just have to pick something up."

The peddler nodded, his thin face drawn with more than the cold and the damp. "Well, you be careful. The Mwellrets aren't to be trusted. You know what they say about them. Look into their eyes, and you belong to them. They steal your soul. They aren't human and they aren't of a human disposition. I never go there. Never."

He went back to eating his meal, and while he finished, no one spoke again. But when he put his plate aside and picked up his cup of ale again, Kimber filled it anew and said, "You've never had any dealings with them?"

"Once," he answered softly. "An accident. They took everything I had and cast me out to die. But I knew the country, so I was able to make my way back home. Never went near them again, not at Dun Fee Aran and not on the road. They're monsters."

He paused. "Let me tell you something about Dun Fee Aran, since you're going there. Haven't told this to anyone. Didn't have a reason and didn't think anyone would believe me, anyway. But you should know. I was inside those walls. They held me there while they decided what to do with me after taking my wares and mule. I saw things. Shades, drifting through the walls as if the stone were nothing more than air. I saw my mother, dead fifteen years. She beckoned to me, tried to lead me out of there. But I couldn't go with her because I couldn't pass through the walls like she could. It's true. I swear it. There was others, too. Things I don't want to talk about. They were there at Dun Fee Aran. The rets didn't seem to see them. Or maybe they didn't care."

He shook his head. "You don't want to go inside those walls again once you've gotten out of them."

His voice trailed off and he stared out into the darkness as if searching for more substantial manifestations of the memories he couldn't quite escape. Fear reflected in his eyes with a bright glitter that warned of the damage such memories could do. He did not seem a cowardly man, or a superstitious one, but in the night's liquid shadows he had clearly found demons other men would never even notice.

"Do you believe me?" he asked quietly.

Jair's mouth was dry and his throat tight in the momentary silence that followed. "I don't know," he said.

The man nodded. "It would be wise if you did."

INDOMITABLE

AT DAWN, the peddler took his leave. They watched him lead his mule through the trees and turn north along the Silver River. Like one of the shades he claimed to have seen in the dungeons at Dun Fee Aran, he walked into the wall of early-morning mist and faded away.

They traveled all that day through country grown thick with scrub and old growth and layered in gray blankets of brume. The world was empty and still, a place in which dampness and gloom smothered all life and left the landscape a tangled wilderness. If not for the Silver River's slender thread, they might easily have lost their way. Even Cogline paused more than once to consider their path. The sky had disappeared into the horizon and the horizon into the earth, so that the land took on the look and feel of a cocoon. Or a coffin. It closed about them and refused to release its death grip. It embraced them with the chilly promise of a constancy that came only with an end to life. Its desolation was both depressing and scary and did nothing to help Jair's already eroded confidence. Bad enough that the peddler had chilled what little fire remained in his determination to continue on; now the land would suffocate the coals as well.

Cogline and Kimber said little to him as they walked, locked away with their own thoughts in the shadowy coverings of their cloaks and hoods, wraiths in the mist. They led their horses like weary warriors come home from war, bent over by exhaustion and memories, lost in dark places. It was a long, slow journey that day, and at times Jair was so certain of the futility of its purpose that he wanted to stop his companions and tell them that they should turn back. It was only the shame he felt at his own weakness that kept him from doing so. He could not expose that weakness, could not admit to it. Should he do so, he knew, he might as well die.

They slept by the river that night, finding a copse of fir that sheltered and concealed them, tethering the horses close by and setting a watch. There was no fire. They were too close to Dun Fee Aran for that. Dinner was eaten cold, ale was consumed to help ward against the chill, and they went to sleep sullen and conflicted.

They woke cold and stiff from the night and the steady drizzle. Within a mile of their camp they found clearer passage along the riverbank, remounted and rode on into the afternoon until, with night descending and an icy wind beginning to blow down out of the mountains, they came in sight of their goal.

It was not a welcome moment. Dun Fee Aran rose before them in a mass of walls and towers, wreathed in mist and shrouded by rain. Torchlight flickered off the rough surfaces of ironbound gates and through the narrow slits of barred windows as if trapped souls were struggling to breathe.

Smoke rose in tendrils from the sputtering flames, giving the keep the look of a smoldering ruin. There was no sign of life, not even shadows cast by moving figures. Nor did any sounds emanate from within. It was as if the keep had been abandoned to the gloom and the peddler's ghosts. The three travelers walked their horses back into the trees some distance away and dismounted. They stood close together as the night descended and the darkness deepened, watching and waiting for something to reveal itself. It was a futile effort.

Jair stared at the keep's forbidding bulk with certain knowledge of what waited within and felt his skin crawl.

"You can't go in there," Kimber said to him suddenly, her voice thin and strained.

"I have to."

"You don't have to do anything. Let this go. I can smell the evil in this place. I taste it on the air." She took hold of his arm. "That peddler was right. Only ghosts belong here. Grandfather, tell him he doesn't have to go any farther with this."

Jair looked at Cogline. The old man met his gaze, then turned away. He had decided to leave it up to the Valeman. It was the first time since they had met that he had taken a neutral stance on the matter of the Ildatch. It spoke volumes about his feelings, now that Dun Fee Aran lay before them.

Jair took a deep breath and looked back at Kimber. "I came a long way for nothing if I don't at least try."

She looked out into the rain and darkness to where the Mwellret castle hunkered down in the shadow of the mountains and shook her head. "I don't care. I didn't know it would be like this. This place feels much worse than I thought it would. I told you before—I don't want anything to happen to you. This"—she gestured toward the fortress—"looks too difficult for anyone."

"It looks abandoned."

She gave him a withering look. "Don't be stupid. You don't believe that. You know what's in there. Why are you even pretending it might be something else?" Her lips compressed in a tight line. "Let's go back. Right now. Let someone else deal with the Ildatch, someone better able. Jair, it's too much!"

There was a desperation in her voice that threatened to drain him of what small resolve he had left. Something of the peddler's fear reflected now in her eyes, a hint of dark places and darker feelings. She was reacting to the visceral feel of Dun Fee Aran, to its hardness and impenetrability, to its ponderous bulk and immutability. She wasn't a coward, but she was intimidated. He couldn't blame her. He could barely bring himself to consider going inside. It was easier to consider simply walking away.

He looked around, as if he might be doing exactly that. "It's too late to go anywhere tonight. Let's make camp back in the trees, where there's some shelter. Let's eat something and get some sleep. We'll think about what to do. We'll decide in the morning."

She seemed to accept that. Without pursuing the matter further, she led the way into the woods, beyond sight and sound of the fortress and its hidden inhabitants, beyond whatever might choose to go abroad.

The rain continued to fall and the wind to blow, the unpleasant mix chasing away any possibility of even the smallest of comforts. They found a windbreak within a stand of fir, the best they could expect, tethered and unsaddled their horses, and settled in.

Their stores were low, and Jair surprised the girl and her grandfather by bringing out an aleskin he told them he had been saving for this moment. They would drink it now, a small indulgence to celebrate their safe arrival and to ward against bad feelings and worse weather. He poured liberally into their cups and watched them drink, being careful only to pretend to drink from his own.

His duplicity troubled him. But he was serving what he perceived to be a greater good, and in his mind that justified far worse.

They were asleep within minutes, stretched out on the forest earth. The medication he had stolen from Kimber and added to the ale had done its job. He unrolled their blankets, wrapped them tightly about, tucked them in under the sheltering fir boughs, and left them to sleep. He had watched Kimber administer the drug to her grandfather each night since they had set out from Hearthstone, his plans already made. If he had judged correctly the measure he had dropped into their ale, they would not wake before morning.

By then, he would be either returned or dead.

He strapped on his short sword, stuck a dagger in his boot, wrapped himself in his greatcoat, and set off to find out which it would be.

H E   D I D   not feel particularly brave or confident about what he had decided to do. Mostly, he felt resigned. Even if Kimber thought he had a choice in the matter, he did not. Jair was not the kind to walk away from his responsibilities, and it didn't matter whether he had asked for them or not. The shade of Allanon had summoned him deliberately and with specific intent. He could not ignore what that meant. He had raveled this path before in his short life, and by doing so he had come to understand a basic truth that others might choose to ignore, but he could not. If he failed to act, it was all too likely no one else would, either.

In his mind, the matter had been decided almost from the outset, and his doubts and fears were simply a testing of his determination.

INDOMITABLE

He took some comfort in the fact that he had managed to keep Kimber and her grandfather from coming with him. They would have done so, of course, well meaning and perhaps even helpful. But he would have worried for them, and that would have rendered his efforts less effective. Besides, it would be all he could do to conceal himself from discovery. To conceal two others while gaining entry into Dun Fee Aran was taking on too much.

Mist and rain obscured his vision, and he was forced to make his way cautiously, unable to see more than a few yards in any direction. Ahead, the dull yellow glow of Dun Fee Aran's torches reflected through the gloom as through a gauzy veil. Beneath his boots, the ground was spongy and littered with deadwood and leaves knocked down by the wind. The air was cold and smelled of damp earth and wet bark. The sharp tang of burning pitch cut through both, a guide to his destination.

Then the trees opened before him, and the massive walls of the fortress came into view, black and shimmering in the rain and mist. He slowed to a walk, studying the parapets and windows carefully, searching for movement. He was already singing, calling up the magic of the wishsong. Unlike Brin, he welcomed it as he would an old friend. Perhaps that had something to do with why he was the one who was here.

Ahead, the main gates to the keep loomed, thick oak timbers wrapped in iron and standing well over twenty feet high. A forbidding obstacle, but he had already seen the smaller door to one side, the one that would be used to admit a traveler on nights such as this when it was too dangerous to chance opening the larger gates. He walked toward that door, still singing, no longer cloaking himself in invisibility but in the pretense of being someone he wasn't.

Slowly, he began to take shape, to assume the form that would gain him entry.

When he reached the smaller doors, he sent a whispered summons to the sentry standing watch inside. He never doubted that someone was there. Like Kimber, he could feel the evil in this place and knew that its source never slept. It took only moments for a response. A slot opened in the iron facing, and yellow-slitted eyes peered out. What they saw wasn't really there. What they saw was another Mwellret, drenched and angry and cloaked in an authority that was not to be challenged. A decision was quickly reached, the door swung outward with a groan of rusted hinges, and a reptilian face appeared in the opening.

"Sstate what bringss..."

The sentry choked hard on the rest of what he was going to ask. The Mwellret he had expected was no longer there. What waited instead was a black-cloaked form that stood seven feet tall and had been thought dead for more than two years.

What the sentry found waiting was the Druid Allanon.

It was a bold gamble on Jair's part, but it had the desired effect. Hissing in fear and loathing, the sentry stumbled backward into the gatehouse, too traumatized even to think to resecure the doors. Jair stepped through at once, forcing the Mwellret to retreat even farther into the small gatehouse. Belatedly, the ret snatched at a pike, but a single threatening gesture was sufficient to cause him to drop the pike in terror and back away once more, this time all the way to the wall.

"You hide a fragment of the Ildatch," the Druid's voice thundered out of Jair. "Give it to me!"

The Mwellret bolted through the back door of the gatehouse into the interior of Dun Fee Aran, crying out as he went, his sibilant voice hoarse before he reached the central tower and disappeared inside. He did not bother to look back to see if Allanon was following, too intent on escaping, on giving warning, on finding help from any quarter. Had he done so, he would have found that the Druid had vanished and the Mwellret he had thought to admit in the first place had reappeared. Cloaked in his new disguise, Jair pursued the fleeing sentry with an intensity that did not allow for distraction. When other rets scurried past him, bound for the gatehouse and the threat that no longer existed, he either stepped back into the shadows or gave way in deference, a lesser to superiors, of no interest or concern to them.

Then he was inside the main stronghold, working his way along hallways and down stairs, swimming upriver against a sudden flow of traffic. The entire fortress had come alive in a swarm of reptilian forms, a nest of vipers with cold, gimlet eyes. *Don't look into those eyes!* He knew the stories of how they stole away men's minds. He had been a victim of their hypnotic effect once and did not intend to be so ever again. He avoided the looks cast his way as the Mwellrets passed, advancing deeper into the keep, leaving behind the shouts and cries that now came mostly from the main courtyard.

He felt time and chance pressing in on him like collapsing walls. Where was the sentry?

He found him not far ahead, gasping out his news to another Mwellret, one that looked to be a good deal more capable of dealing with the unexpected. This second ret listened without comment, dispatched the frightened sentry back the way he had come, and turned down a corridor that led still deeper into the keep. Jair, mustering his courage, followed.

His quarry moved with purpose along the corridor and then down a winding set of stairs. He glanced back once or twice, but by now Jair had changed his appearance again, no longer another Mwellret, but a part of the fortress itself. He was the walls, the floor, the air, and nothing at all. The Mwellret might look over his shoulder as many times as he chose, but he would have to look carefully to realize that there was something wrong with what he was seeing.

But what concerned Jair was that the ret might not be leading him to the Ildatch fragment after all. He had assumed that the sentry would rush to give warning of the threat from Allanon and by doing so lead Jair to those who guarded the page fragment he had come to destroy. Yet there was nothing to indicate

that the ret was taking him to where he wanted to go. If he had guessed wrong about this, he was going to have trouble of a sort he didn't care to contemplate. His ability to employ the magic was not inexhaustible. Sooner or later, he would tire. Then he would be left not only exposed, but also defenseless.

Torchlight flooded the corridor ahead. An iron-bound door and guards holding massive pikes blocked the way forward. The Mwellret he followed signaled perfunctorily to the watch as he stepped out of the darkened corridor into the light, and the guards released the locks and stepped aside for him. Jair, still invisible to those around him, took advantage of the change of light, closed swiftly on his quarry at the entry, and slipped into the chamber behind him just as the door swung closed again.

Standing just inside, he glanced quickly at the cavernous, smoke-filled chamber and its occupants. Seven, no eight, Mwellrets clustered about a huge wooden table on which rested bottles, vials, and similar containers amid a scattering of old books and tablets. At their center, carefully placed on a lectern that kept it raised above everything, was a single piece of aged paper, its edges burned and curled. A strange glow emanated from that fragment, and the writing on its worn surface pulsed steadily. The aura it gave off was so viscerally repellent that Jair recoiled in spite of himself, a sudden wave of nausea flooding through him.

There was no question in his mind about what he was seeing. Forcing his repulsion aside, he gathered up the fraying threads of his determination and threw the bolt that locked the door from the inside.

Nine heads turned as one, scaly faces lifting into the light from out of shadowy hoods. A moment of uncertainty rooted the Mwellrets in place, and then the one the Valeman had followed down from the upper halls started back for the door, a long knife appearing in his clawed hand. Jair was already moving sideways, skirting the edges of the chamber, heading for the table and its contents. The Mwellrets had begun to move forward, placing themselves between the door and their prize, their attention focused on what might be happening outside in the hallway. All the Valeman needed was a few moments to get behind them and seize the page. He could feed it into one of the torches before they could stop him. If he were quick enough, they would never even realize he was there.

INDOMITABLE

Stay calm. Don't rush. Don't give yourself away.

The Mwellret at the entry released the lock and wrenched open the door. The startled sentries turned in surprise as he looked past them wordlessly into the corridor beyond, searching. Jair had reached the table and was sliding along its edge toward the page fragment, a clear path ahead of him. The Mwellrets were muttering now, glancing about uneasily, trying to decide if they were threatened or not. He had only a few seconds left.

He reached the lectern, snatched up the page fragment, and dropped it with a howl as it burned his fingers like a live coal.

Instantly the Mwellrets swung around, watching their precious relic gutter in the air before settling back on the table amid the debris, steaming and writhing like a living thing. Shouts rose from its protectors, some snatching out blades from beneath their cloaks and beginning to fan out across the chamber. Furious with himself, terrified by his failure, Jair backed away, fighting to stay calm. Magic warded the Ildatch fragment as it had warded the book itself. Whether this was magic of the book's own making or of its keepers, it changed what was required. If he couldn't hold the page, how was he going to feed it into the fire? How was he going to destroy it?

He backed against the wall, sliding away from the searching rets, who were still uncertain what they were looking for. They knew something was there, but they didn't know what. If he could keep them guessing long enough...

His mind raced, his fading possibilities skittering about like rats in a cage.

Then one of the Mwellrets, perhaps guessing at his subterfuge, snatched up a round wooden container from the table, reached into it, and began tossing out handfuls of white powder. Everything the powder settled on, it coated. Jair knew what was coming. Once the powder was flung in his direction, he would be outlined as clearly as if a shadow cast in bright sunlight. The best he could hope for was to find a way to destroy the Ildatch fragment before that happened, and he was likely to get only one more chance.

He glanced over his shoulder to where a torch burned in its wall mount behind him. If he snatched it up and rushed forward, he could lay it against the paper. That should be enough to finish the matter.

Steady. Don't rush.

The Mwellrets were moving back around the table now, hands groping the empty air as they attempted to flush out their invisible intruder. The Mwellret with the powder continued to toss handfuls into the air, but he was still on the other side of the table and not yet close enough to threaten. The Valeman kept the wishsong steady and his concentration focused as he edged closer to his goal. What he needed was another distraction, a small window of opportunity to act.

Then the ret with the powder turned abruptly and began throwing handfuls in his direction.

The immediacy of the threat proved too much for the Valeman to endure. He reacted instinctively, abandoning the magic that cloaked him in the appearance of invisibility for something stronger. Images of Garet Jax flooded the room, black cloaked forms wielding blades in both hands and moving like seasoned fighters. It was all Jair could come up with in his welter of panic and need, and he grasped at it as a drowning man would a lifeline.

At first, it appeared it would be enough. The Mwellrets fell back in terror, caught off guard, unprepared for so many adversaries appearing all at once. Even the sentries who now blocked the doorway retreated, pikes lifting defensively. Whatever magic was at work, it was beyond anything with which they were familiar, and they did not know what to do about it.

It was the distraction Jair required, and he took immediate advantage of it. He reached for one of the torches set in wall brackets behind him, grasped it by the handle, and wrenched at it. But his hands were coated in sweat and he could not pull it loose from its fitting. The Mwellrets hissed furiously, seeing him clearly now behind his wall of protectors, realizing at once what he intended. Under different circumstances, they might have hesitated longer before acting, but they were driven by an irrational and overwhelming need to protect the Ildatch fragment. Whatever else they might countenance, they would not stand by and lose their chance at immortality.

They came at the images of Garet Jax in a swarm, wielding their knives and short swords in a glittering frenzy, slashing and hacking without regard for their own safety. The fury and suddenness of their onslaught caught Jair by surprise, and his concentration faltered. One by one, his images disappeared. The Mwellrets found not real warriors facing them, but men made of little more than colored vapor.

INDOMITABLE

The Valeman gave up on his effort to free the recalcitrant torch and turned to face the Mwellrets. They were all around him and closing in, their blades forming a circle of sharp-edged steel that he could not get past. He had been too slow, too hesitant. His chance was gone. Despairing, he drew his own sword to defend himself. He thought fleetingly of Garet Jax, trying to remember the way he had moved when surrounded by his enemies, trying to imagine what he might do now.

And as if in response, a fresh image formed, unbidden and wholly unexpected. In a shimmer of dark air, the Weapons Master reappeared, a replication of the images already destroyed, black-cloaked and wielding one of the deadly blades he had carried in life. But this image did not separate itself from Jair as the others had. Instead, it closed about him like a second skin. It happened so fast that the Valeman did not have time to try to stop it.

In seconds, he had become the image.

Instantly, this hybrid version of himself joined to the Weapons Master vaulted into the Mwellrets with a singlemindedness of purpose that was breathtaking. The rets, thinking it harmless, barely brushed at it with their weapons. Two of them died for their carelessness in a single pass. Another fell on a lunge that buried his blade so deep it had to be wrenched free. Belatedly, the Mwellrets realized they were faced with something new. They slashed and cut with their own blades in retaliation, but they might as well have been wielding wooden toys. Jair heard sharp intakes of breath as his knives found their mark; he felt the shudder of bodies and the thrashing of limbs. Mwellrets stumbled, dying on their feet, stunned looks on their faces as he swept through them, killing with scythelike precision.

It was horrific and exhilarating, and the Valeman was immersed in it, living it. For a few stunning moments, he was someone else entirely, someone whose thoughts and experiences were not his own. He wasn't just watching Garet Jax—he *was* Garet Jax. He was so lost to himself, so much a part of the Weapons Master, that even though what he was experiencing was dark and scary, it filled him with satisfaction and a deep longing for more.

Now the ret guards rushed to join the battle, pikes spearing at him. The guards were trained and not so easily dispatched. A hooked point sliced through his sword arm, sending a flash of jagged pain into his

body. He feinted and sidestepped the next thrust. The guards cut at him, but he was ready now and eluded them easily. A phantom sliding smoothly beneath each sweep of their weapons, he was inside their killing arc and on top of them before they realized they had failed to stop him.

Seconds later, the last of the rets lay lifeless on the floor.

But when he wheeled back to survey the devastation he had left in his wake, he saw the young Valeman who had remained on the far side of the table. Their eyes met, and he felt something shift inside. The Valeman was fading away even as he watched, turning slowly transparent, becoming a ghost.

He was disappearing.

Do something!

He snatched free a torch mounted on the wall behind him and threw it into the powders and potions on the table. Instantly, the volatile mix went up in flames, white hot and spitting. The Ildatch fragment pulsed at its center, then rose from the table into the scorched air, riding the back of invisible currents generated by the heat.

Escaping...

INDOMITABLE

He snatched the dagger from his boot and leapt forward, spearing the hapless scrap of paper in mid-air and pinning it to the wooden tabletop where the flames were fiercest. The paper curled against his skin in a clutching motion and his head snapped back in shock as razor-sharp pains raced up his arm and into his chest. But he refused to let go. Ignoring the pain, he held the paper pinned in place. When the inferno finally grew so intense that he was forced to release his death grip on the dagger and back away, the Ildatch fragment was just barely recognizable. He stood clutching his seared hand on the far side of the burning table, watching the scrap of paper slowly wither and turn to dust.

Then he walked back around the table and through the image of the Valeman and he was inside his own body again. Feeling as if a weight had been lifted from his shoulders, he looked over to where the shadowy, black-cloaked figure he had been joined to was fading away, returning to the ether from which it had come, returning to the land of the dead.

HE FLED the chamber, skittering through the sprawl of Mwellret bodies and out the door, hugging the walls of the smoke-filled corridors and stairwells that led to safety. His mind spun with images of what he had just experienced, leaving him unsteady and riddled with doubt. Despite having the use of the wishsong to disguise his passing, he felt completely exposed.

What had happened back there?

Had Garet Jax found a way to come back from the dead on his own, choosing to be Jair's protector one final time? Had Allanon sent him through a trick of Druid magic that transcended the dictates of the grave?

Perhaps.

But Jair didn't think so. What he thought was that he alone was responsible, that somehow the wishsong had given that last image life.

It was impossible, but that was what he believed.

He took deep, slow breaths to steady himself as he climbed out of Dun Fee Aran's prisons. It was madness to think that his magic could give life to the dead. It suggested possibilities that he could only just bear to consider. Giving life to the dead violated all of nature's laws. It made his skin crawl.

INDOMITABLE

But it had saved him, hadn't it? It had enabled him to destroy the Ildatch fragment, and that was what he had come to Dun Fee Aran to do. What difference did it make how it had been accomplished?

Yet it did make a difference. He remembered how it had felt to be a part of Garet Jax. He remembered how it had felt to kill those Mwellrets, to hear their frantic cries, to see their stricken looks, to smell their blood and fear. He remembered the grating of his blade against their bones and the surprisingly soft yield of their scaly flesh. He hadn't hated it; he had enjoyed it—enough so that for the brief moments he had been connected to the Weapons Master, he had craved it. Even now, in the terrible, blood-drenched aftermath when his thoughts and body were his own again, he hungered for more.

What if he had not looked back at the last moment and seen himself fading away?

What if he had not sensed the unexpectedly dangerous position he had placed himself in, joined to a ghost out of time?

He found his way up from the prisons more easily than he had expected he would, moving swiftly and smoothly through the chaos. He did not encounter any more Mwellrets until he reached the upper halls, where they were clustered in angry bands, still looking for something that wasn't there, still unaware that the Druid they sought was an illusion. Perhaps the sounds had been muffled by the stone walls and iron doors, but they had not discovered yet what had happened belowground. They did not see him as he passed, cloaked in his magic, and in moments, he was back at the gates. Distracting the already distracted guards long enough to open the door one last time, he melted into the night.

He walked from the fortress through the rain and mist, using the wishsong until he reached the trees, then stopped, the magic dying on his lips. His knees gave way, and he sat on the damp ground and stared into space. His burned hand throbbed and the wound to his arm ached. He was alive, but he felt dead inside. Still, how he felt inside was his own fault. Wasn't bringing Garet Jax back from the dead what he had wanted all along? Wasn't that the purpose of preserving all those memories of Graymark and the Croagh? To make the past he so greatly prized a part of the present?

He placed his hand against the cool earth and stared at it.

Something wasn't right.

If it was the Weapons Master who had fought against the Mwellrets and destroyed the fragment of the Ildatch, why was his hand burned? Why was his arm wounded?

He stared harder, remembering. Garet Jax had carried only one blade in his battle with the Mwellrets, rather than the two all of the other images had carried.

Jair's blade.

His throat tightened in shock. He was looking at this all wrong. The wishsong hadn't brought Garet Jax back from the dead. It hadn't brought Garet Jax back at all. There was only one of them in that charnel house tonight.

Himself.

He saw the truth of things now, all of it, what he had so completely misread. Brin had warned him not to trust the magic, had cautioned him that it was dangerous. But he had ignored her. He had assumed that because his use of it was different from her own, less potent and seemingly more harmless, it did not threaten in the same way. She could actually change things, could create or destroy, whereas he could only give the appearance of doing so. Where was the harm in that?

But his magic had evolved. Perhaps it had done so because he had grown. Perhaps it was just the natural consequence of time's passage. Whatever the case, sometime in the past two years it had undergone a terrible transformation. And tonight in the dungeons of Dun Fee Aran, responding to the unfamiliar urgency of his desperation and fear, it had revealed its new capabilities for the first time.

He hadn't conjured up the shade of Garet Jax. He hadn't given life to a dead man in some mysterious way. What he had done was to remake himself in the Weapons Master's image. That had been all him back there, cloaked in his once-protector's trappings, a replica of the killing machine the other had been. That was why he had felt everything so clearly, why it had all seemed so real. It was. The Garet Jax in the chambers of Dun Fee Aran was a reflection of himself, of his own dark nature, of what lay buried just beneath the surface.

A reflection, he recalled with a chill, into which he had almost disappeared completely.

Because risking that fate was necessary if he was to survive and the Ildatch to be destroyed.

Then a further revelation came to him, one so terrible that he knew almost as soon as it occurred to him that it was true. Allanon had known what his magic would do when he had summoned him through Cogline's dreams. Allanon had known that it would surface to protect him against the Mwellrets.

Kimber Boh had been right. The Druid had used him. Even in death, it could still manipulate the living. Circumstances required it, necessity dictated it, and Jair was sacrificed to both at the cost of a glimpse into the blackest part of his soul.

He closed his eyes against what he was feeling. He wanted to go home. He wanted to forget everything that had happened this night. He wanted to bury the knowledge of what his magic could do. He wanted never to have come this way.

He ran his fingers through the damp leaves and rain-softened earth at his feet, stirring up the pungent smells of both, tracing idle patterns as he waited for his feelings to settle and his head to clear. Somewhere in the distance, he heard fresh cries from the fortress. They had discovered the chamber where the dead men lay. They would try to understand what had happened, but would not be able to do so.

Only he would ever know.

After long moments, he opened his eyes again and brushed the dirt and debris off his injured hand. He would return to Kimber and her grandfather and wake them. He would tell them some of what had happened, but not all. He might never tell anyone all of it.

He wondered if he would heed his sister's advice and never use the magic again. He wondered what would happen if he chose to ignore that advice again or if fate and circumstances made it impossible for him to do otherwise, as had happened tonight. He wondered what the consequences would be next time.

The past is always with us, but sometimes we don't recognize it right away for what it is.

He got to his feet and started walking.